Whose Club Is Better?

"We're going to find an orchid name for you, too," Ellen said.

Elizabeth looked surprised. "I don't want an orchid name. Didn't Jessica tell you? I'm not joining your club."

Jessica felt embarrassed. She wished Elizabeth would go away.

"I'm in my own club," Elizabeth said. "Anyone can be in it without needing any stupid silk flower."

"I think the Sunflower Club is stupid," Jessica blurted out angrily.

Elizabeth frowned. "It is not, Jess."

"My name is Vanilla!" Jessica shouted.

Elizabeth looked as if she might start to cry.

Bantam Skylark Books in the SWEET VALLEY KIDS series

SWEET VALLEY KIDS

JESSICA'S SNOBBY CLUB

Written by
Molly Mia Stewart

Created by
FRANCINE PASCAL

Illustrated by
Ying-Hwa Hu

A BANTAM SKYLARK BOOK®
NEW YORK · TORONTO · LONDON · SYDNEY · AUCKLAND

RL 2, 005–008

JESSICA'S SNOBBY CLUB
A Bantam Skylark Book / February 1992

Sweet Valley High® and Sweet Valley Kids are
trademarks of Francine Pascal

Conceived by Francine Pascal
Produced by Daniel Weiss Associates, Inc.
33 West 17th Street
New York, NY 10011

Cover art by Susan Tang

Skylark Books is a registered trademark of Bantam Books, a
division of Bantam Doubleday Dell Publishing Group, Inc.
Registered in U.S. Patent and Trademark Office and elsewhere.

ISBN 0-553-15922-4

Published simultaneously in the United States and Canada

Bantam Books are published by Bantam Books, a division of Bantam
Doubleday Dell Publishing Group, Inc. Its trademark, consisting of the
words "Bantam Books" and the portrayal of a rooster, is Registered in
U.S. Patent and Trademark Office and in other countries. Marca Regis-
trada. Bantam Books, 1540 Broadway, New York, New York 10036.

PRINTED IN THE UNITED STATES OF AMERICA
CWO   0 9 8 7 6 5 4

*To the children of
Rosie and Harry's Place*

CHAPTER 1

Gifts from Hawaii

"I made up a new poem," Elizabeth Wakefield told her twin sister, Jessica, as they walked home from school. "Violets are blue, roses are pink, it's almost Valentine's Day, I think."

Jessica shook her head and laughed. "That's dumb, Liz."

"I know, but it's funny," Elizabeth said. "It made you laugh, didn't it?"

Elizabeth enjoyed making up poems. Of all the subjects in second grade, she loved reading and writing the best. Whenever she read a book, she imagined herself as one of the characters. But reading wasn't the only thing she liked to do. She also enjoyed playing outside, and she was proud to be in the Sweet Valley Soccer League.

Jessica was just the opposite. She didn't like reading or writing very much, and she preferred to play inside most of the time. Her favorite after-school activities were going to her dance lessons and playing with her dolls and stuffed animals.

Everyone was always surprised that identical twins could have such different personalities. After all, Elizabeth and Jessica looked exactly alike, so it was easy to think they were the same on the inside, too. Both girls had blue-green eyes and long blond hair with bangs.

No matter how different they were,

though, Elizabeth and Jessica were best friends. They shared everything, and each twin often seemed to know what the other was thinking.

"I'm starving for a snack," Elizabeth said as she and Jessica walked into the house together. Mrs. Wakefield called out to them from the kitchen, where she was doing homework for her decorating class.

"Hi, Mom," Jessica said, putting her books down next to a stack of wallpaper samples. "Hey, what's this?" She picked up a package wrapped in brown paper.

"Something from Hawaii," Mrs. Wakefield answered. She smiled mysteriously. "I wonder what it could be."

"It must be from Grandma and Grandpa," Elizabeth said. "I bet they're having a great vacation."

3

Jessica giggled. "I wonder if Grandma is learning the hula-hula dance." She shook the package. "Look, it has my name on it."

Elizabeth glanced at the table. She saw another package addressed to their older brother, Steven. But there wasn't a package with her name on it.

"Is it a Valentine's Day present?" Elizabeth asked. Valentine's Day was four days away. Grandma and Grandpa Wakefield always gave each of them a present, so she was surprised not to see one for her.

"Honey, I called Grandma and Grandpa," Mrs. Wakefield said. "I knew they must have sent you something, too. We think it must be held up in the mail. Don't worry. I'm sure it'll arrive tomorrow or the day after."

Elizabeth shrugged. She knew her grandparents would never forget to send her a present. And since the twins were usually given identical gifts, she knew that when her Valentine's Day present arrived, it would be the same as Jessica's.

"Go ahead and open it," Elizabeth said to Jessica.

Jessica didn't wait another second. She ripped open the brown paper and took out a small box wrapped in pink foil. "Wow," she said, as she took the lid off the box. "It's a silk orchid!"

"Let me see." Elizabeth leaned over for a closer look.

Inside the box was a beautiful pink and white cloth flower. Elizabeth could see that it was a pin.

"I always wanted one of these," Jessica said, taking the orchid pin out. "Lila's dad got two of them for her when he went to

Hawaii last summer, and Lila was supposed to give one to me."

Elizabeth knew the whole story. Lila Fowler, who was Jessica's best friend after Elizabeth, often received fancy presents from her rich father. When Lila first got her silk orchids, she had promised to give one to Jessica. But Jessica was sick on the day she was supposed to go to Lila's house after school. Ellen Riteman went to Lila's house that day instead, and Ellen had had the second orchid ever since.

"Now I have one, too," Jessica said happily as she pinned the orchid to her shirt. "Wait until Lila and Ellen see it!"

Elizabeth laughed. She knew Jessica was going to talk about only one thing now—the orchid. She couldn't wait for the mailman to deliver hers.

CHAPTER 2

The Orchid Club

Jessica walked into Mrs. Otis's classroom the next day with a proud smile on her face. She saw Lila and Ellen sitting together. Lila was showing off a pen that could write in six different colors.

"Notice anything new?" Jessica asked, sitting down next to her friends.

Lila and Ellen both stared at her. "Hey!" Lila said. "You have a silk orchid! Where did you get it?"

"It's a Valentine's Day present from my grandparents. It came all the way from Hawaii," Jessica said proudly.

"It's just like ours," Ellen said. "I have an idea. Let's all wear our orchids tomorrow."

"I bet we're the only girls in school with silk orchids," Lila said confidently. "We could be a club."

Jessica leaned forward with an excited look in her eyes. "That's a great idea!" she said. "We can call ourselves the Orchid Club."

"Only girls with silk orchids can be in it," Ellen said.

"The three of us," Lila said.

"And Liz," Jessica added quickly.

"Did she get one, too?" Ellen asked.

"No, but she will," Jessica explained. "Hers got lost in the mail, but it's on the way."

Lila folded her arms. "If she doesn't have

10

an orchid, she can't be in the Orchid Club."

"But she *will* have an orchid," Jessica insisted, looking from Lila to Ellen and back again. "Our grandparents always send us the same present."

Lila shook her head. "If she doesn't have one *now*, she can't be in the club."

Jessica sat back in her chair and frowned. She didn't think it was right for Elizabeth to be left out just because her present was late. Jessica and Elizabeth did almost everything together, and Jesisca wasn't sure she wanted to be in a club without her sister. She would have to convince Lila and Ellen that Elizabeth should be allowed to join. "I'll be right back," she said.

Jessica got up and hurried across the

room. Elizabeth was feeding the class hamsters, Tinkerbell and Thumbelina. "You have to explain something to Lila and Ellen," Jessica told her sister.

"What?" Elizabeth asked. She held a sunflower seed between her fingers for Tinkerbell to nibble.

"We're starting a club called the Orchid Club," Jessica said. "They say you can't be in it because you don't have an orchid. I told them yours would be here soon."

Elizabeth dusted off her hands. "So?" she asked.

"So, tell them you want to be in it," Jessica said.

"Maybe I don't," Elizabeth said. "Who wants to be in a club with such snobby members?"

Jessica frowned. She looked sadly back at

her friends. Having a silk orchid was something she had dreamed of for a long time. Now that she finally had one, she wanted to be in the Orchid Club with Lila and Ellen. But not without Elizabeth.

"I guess I don't want to be in the club," she mumbled, sitting back down with Lila and Ellen.

"But you have to!" Ellen said. "It was your idea. We're going to make up special names and secret rules and everything."

Jessica brightened. "Really?"

"And we'll have special meetings," Lila continued. "Clubs always do."

"Please be in the club with us," Ellen said. "When Elizabeth gets her orchid, then she can be in it, too."

Jessica chewed on her thumbnail and thought. She really did want to be in the club. It would be fun to have secret codes and rules that nobody else knew about. Elizabeth could join as soon as her orchid arrived.

"OK," Jessica said with a big smile. "I'll be in the club."

CHAPTER 3

Sunflowers

The following morning, Elizabeth opened the door to the large walk-in closet that she and Jessica shared. "What are you wearing today?" she asked her sister.

Jessica was rummaging in a dresser drawer. "White shorts and my purple sweater," she said.

"I'll wear my purple sweater, too," Elizabeth decided.

"No!" Jessica blurted out.

Elizabeth looked at her in surprise. "Why not?" she asked.

"It's one of the rules," Jessica told her seriously.

"What rules?" Elizabeth asked. Usually Jessica liked it when they dressed in identical clothes. It was fun watching their friends and teachers try to tell them apart.

"The Orchid Club rules," Jessica said with a worried frown. "We have to wear purple sweaters or shirts to school. Since you're not in the Orchid Club yet, you shouldn't wear the same thing I'm wearing."

Elizabeth pulled her purple sweater off the hanger. "I think that's silly," she said.

"It's not silly," Jessica insisted. "We can't dress the same for a while, until your orchid comes and you join the club."

Thinking about the Orchid Club made Elizabeth feel stubborn. "I'm wearing what I want to," she said. "And today I want to wear my purple sweater."

Jessica watched her get dressed without saying a word.

When Elizabeth was finished, she walked out of their bedroom and went downstairs for breakfast.

"Good morning, sweetheart," Mr. Wakefield said cheerfully.

Elizabeth sat down at the table and stared into her glass of orange juice. "Good morning," she replied quietly.

When Jessica had first told her about the Orchid Club, Elizabeth had thought it was just another one of Lila's stuck-up ideas. It was nothing to get upset about. Now that Jessica was taking the rules so seriously, though, Elizabeth was beginning to feel left out.

"Good morning, Jessica," Mr. Wakefield said.

Elizabeth glanced up as her sister sat down next to her. Jessica was not wearing her purple sweater. Instead, she had put on a purple T-shirt. Her silk orchid was pinned on the front.

Elizabeth felt even worse. She was afraid that the Orchid Club was taking away her best friend.

"What do they do in the club?" Amy Sutton asked Elizabeth during recess.

Elizabeth bounced Amy's small rubber ball a few times before she answered. "Just make up rules, I guess."

Eva Simpson laughed. "That doesn't sound like much fun," she said. She was drawing a sunflower on the back of her hand with a marking pen.

Elizabeth looked across the playground to where Jessica, Lila, and Ellen were sitting by themselves, deep in conversation. "It really makes me mad that they won't let anyone who doesn't have a silk orchid join," she said. "It's such a stupid reason."

"I know what you mean," Eva said. "I guess I'll never be an Orchid."

"I wouldn't want to be one even if I could," Amy said, taking her ball back from Elizabeth and tossing it in the air. "Who wants to climb trees or play tag with a silk flower on? I know I'd ruin it."

"We should start a club that anyone can join," Eva suggested.

Elizabeth nodded. "With no rules," she said.

"All you'd have to do to be in it is ask," Amy went on, tossing up the ball again.

"We could draw sunflowers on our hands," Eva said, showing her friends the one she had drawn on her own hand.

"Yes!" Elizabeth said eagerly. "Let's do that. We can call ourselves the Sunflower Club. Can you draw sunflowers for us, Eva?"

Eva took the cap off her pen. "I sure can," she said, smiling. "Hold out your hands!"

CHAPTER 4

Vanilla Bean

"Look what I have." Lila opened her book bag. Before she reached into it, she looked suspiciously over her shoulder.

"What is it?" Jessica asked, leaning closer. It was recess, and the three members of the Orchid Club were sitting on a bench at the edge of the playground.

"I found a book about orchids in my father's library," Lila said.

"Let me see," Jessica said, reaching for the book.

Lila snatched it away and held it against

her stomach. "Wait a second," she said. "Somebody's coming."

Two girls from their class, Caroline Pearce and Julie Porter, were walking toward them.

"Hi," Caroline said. "We heard about your club. Can we be in it?"

Jessica, Lila, and Ellen exchanged a serious look.

"Do you have silk orchids?" Lila asked.

Caroline shook her head. "I have a glass angelfish."

"I have a silk ribbon," Julie said in a hopeful voice.

"Sorry," Ellen said, shaking her head. "You have to have a silk orchid to be in the Orchid Club."

"Well, Elizabeth is starting a club, too," Caroline said, putting her nose in the air.

"And she's letting in anyone who wants to join. So there."

As Caroline and Julie walked away, Lila let out a sigh of relief. "Whew," she said. "If we let everyone join who wanted to, we'd have a million people."

Jessica wished that Julie had a silk flower so that she could join the Orchids. Julie was one of the nicest girls in the whole second grade. And even though Caroline was a nosy tattletale, it would be fun to have a few more people in the club so they could play more games.

"Well, so far we only have three people," Jessica pointed out. "And it looks as if that's all we'll ever have."

"Until Elizabeth gets her orchid," Ellen reminded her.

Lila nodded. "Right. We have to be picky. Elizabeth is starting a club because she's jealous. But I know she'll join ours as soon as she can."

Jessica wasn't so sure. She knew Elizabeth didn't like to be bossed around, especially by Lila.

"I think we should have special orchid names," Lila continued, opening her book again. "I've already picked them out. My name is Lady's Slipper. Ellen, yours is Moccasin Flower."

"What's my name?" Jessica asked.

"You'll be called Vanilla," Lila said.

Jessica's mouth dropped open. "*Vanilla?*" she repeated. She had been expecting something more exotic and glamorous.

"Vanilla beans come from orchids," Lila said. "Didn't you know that?"

"No," Jessica said, beginning to feel grouchy at Lila's bossy behavior. "I bet you didn't either until you looked in that book."

She looked across the playground. Elizabeth, Amy, and Eva were surrouded by a large group of girls. They seemed to be writing on the backs of each other's hands. Everyone was laughing.

"That must be their club," Jessica said.

Lila made a sour face. "Look, they even let in Lois Waller, the biggest crybaby in the whole school."

While the members of the Orchid Club watched, the girls in the Sunflower Club began a game of freeze tag. Jessica almost wished she could be in Elizabeth's club. They were having fun and playing games. The Orchids didn't even have enough members to play double Dutch jump rope. "Let's play tag with them for a while," she suggested eagerly. "It looks like fun."

"No way!" Lila said with a gasp. "That's their club. We have to stick with ours."

"Then maybe I'll be in that club, too," Jessica grumbled. "At least they get to have fun."

Lila and Ellen looked shocked. "You can't be in both clubs, Jessica," Ellen said. "It's a rule."

"Besides, we're having a secret meeting tomorrow after school," Lila went on mysteriously. "At my house."

As soon as Jessica heard the world "secret," she forgot all about the Sunflower Club. She was dying to know what the secret meeting was about, and the only way to find out was to go to Lila's.

Suddenly she remembered something. "I

promised to go to the library with Liz after school tomorrow," she said.

"The *library*?" Ellen repeated. "I thought you said you wanted to have fun. Going to the library doesn't sound like much fun to me."

Lila tapped her orchid book with one finger. "Jessica, this is important. You can go to the library any old time. If you don't come to the meeting tomorrow, then you can't be in the Orchid Club. You have to go to *all* the meetings. It's a rule, remember?"

Jessica put her chin in her hands. She didn't want to break her promise to Elizabeth. But belonging to a special club with only three members was a special honor. She just couldn't miss the meeting. She was sure that Elizabeth would understand.

CHAPTER 5

Late Delivery

The next afternoon, Elizabeth walked over to the checkout desk of the Sweet Valley Public Library.

"Hello, Elizabeth," said Mrs. Bullard, one of the librarians. "Where's Jessica today?"

"She went over to a friend's house to play," Elizabeth said quietly.

She didn't feel very much like talking to Mrs. Bullard. She didn't even feel like reading her books. Jessica had told her that she had an important reason for going to Lila's house after school instead of to the library. But she wouldn't say what the reason was.

Elizabeth had a pretty good idea, though. She was sure it had something to do with the Orchid Club. All day after recess yesterday, Jessica had kept telling everyone that her new name was "Vanilla." Elizabeth thought that was silly. It seemed as if Jessica was trying to change who she was, just to be in the club. Elizabeth couldn't understand why being in the Orchid Club was so important.

"Stupid Orchid Club," Elizabeth muttered, as she headed outside to where her mother was waiting in the car.

When she got home, Elizabeth sat at her desk and stared at her chimpanzee wall calendar. The next day was Valentine's Day. She slid open a drawer and pulled out a stack of colorful handmade cards. She had made cards for Eva, Amy, Lois, Julie, and all of the other girls in the Sunflower Club. Elizabeth had drawn big yellow sunflowers next to their names. She had also made cards for Todd Wilkins, Ken Matthews, Winston Egbert, and some of the other boys in her class. There was a special card for her teacher, Mrs. Otis, too.

So far, however, she hadn't made a Valentine's Day card for Jessica. Elizabeth always saved Jessica's card for the very last. That way, she could practice drawing hearts on all the other cards, so Jessica's would be the best.

Feeling a little bit sad, Elizabeth picked out a sheet of pink construction paper. She carefully folded it in half and then drew a perfect heart on the front.

"To the best sister in the whole world," Elizabeth wrote inside in her neatest handwriting. "Love, Liz."

Then she closed it. She wished Jessica would get home.

"Elizabeth!" Mrs. Wakefield called from downstairs. "Come see what the mailman just brought!"

Elizabeth quickly put all of the cards back in her desk. Then she hurried downstairs.

"Is it my present?" she asked.

Mrs. Wakefield held out a small package addressed to Elizabeth. "It sure is. The postmark says Hawaii."

"Great!" Elizabeth said, smiling. "It got here just in time for Valentine's Day."

As she began to open the package, the front door opened, and Jessica came in.

"Hi," Jessica said, giving Elizabeth a guilty look. She still felt bad about breaking her promise, even though the Orchid Club

35

meeting had been fun. Then she noticed Elizabeth's package. "What's that?"

"It's from Grandma and Grandpa," Elizabeth said, tearing off the paper.

"It's your orchid!" Jessica said. "I know it is. It has to be!" She was excited. Now Elizabeth could join the club, too. They could start wearing identical outfits again, and doing everything together at recess and after school. Jessica couldn't wait.

Elizabeth didn't say anything. She concentrated on taking off the brown paper and then the pink foil. Then she lifted the lid off the small box.

Jessica clapped her hands when she saw what was inside. "It *is* an orchid! Now you can be in the Orchid Club!"

Elizabeth took the silk orchid pin out of the box and examined it. It was exactly like

Jessica's except that it was light blue instead of pink. It was beautiful.

"Aren't you glad?" Jessica asked happily. "You can be in our club now."

"I don't want to be in your club," Elizabeth answered. "But you can join the Sunflowers any time you want."

CHAPTER 6

Name-Calling

Jessica cut a heart shape from a piece of red paper and glued it onto a paper doily. The whole class was busy making Valentine's Day cards. Jessica could hear people talking cheerfully about the class party that afternoon. Jessica didn't feel very cheerful, though. She wrote "Dad" on the red paper heart in swirly letters with glue.

"Did you see the cupcakes Mrs. Otis made?" Ellen asked her. "They have candy hearts on them. I can't wait for the party."

"Me, neither," Lila said. She looked at the

next table, where Elizabeth was working with Eva and Amy. "Vanilla, did Elizabeth get her orchid yet?"

Jessica sprinkled some silver glitter on the glue.

"Vanilla?" Lila repeated.

"Oh, I forgot that was my name," Jessica said. "Yes, she got it yesterday."

"That's good," Ellen said. "Now she can be in the Orchid Club with us."

"Right," Lila agreed. "Anyone with a silk orchid is automatically in the club." The three of them were wearing their orchid pins, as usual.

Jessica didn't want to admit that Elizabeth didn't want to be in the Orchid Club. She couldn't understand why her own sister would stay out of the club on purpose. Why couldn't Elizabeth understand that being in it was a special honor? Maybe if Jessica told her more about it, Elizabeth would change her mind and join.

"We have to find an orchid name for her," Ellen said. "Did you bring the book today, Lady's Slipper?"

"Of course, Moccasin Flower," Lila said.

Jessica scrunched up her nose. "I don't think Liz would want one of those names."

"Why not?" Ellen asked.

Just then Elizabeth walked over to their table. "Can I borrow that silver glitter, Jessica?" she asked.

"You're supposed to call her Vanilla," Ellen said. "We're going to find an orchid name for you now, too."

Elizabeth looked surprised. "I don't want an orchid name. Didn't Jessica tell you? I'm not joining your club."

"You're not?" Lila asked.

Jessica felt embarrassed. She wished Elizabeth would go away.

"I'm in my own club," Elizabeth said. "Anyone can be in it without needing any stupid silk flower."

"I think the Sunflower Club is stupid," Jessica blurted out angrily.

Elizabeth frowned. "It is not, Jess."

"My name is Vanilla!" Jessica shouted.

Some of the boys who were sitting nearby began to laugh. Jessica felt more embarrassed and upset than ever. Right then and there, she decided not to give Elizabeth the Valentine's Day card she had made for her.

Elizabeth looked as if she might start to cry. She picked up the silver glitter and walked quickly back to the other table.

"What's wrong with her?" Lila asked.

"Nothing," Jessica muttered. "She's too stuck-up to be in our club, that's all."

Even while she said it, Jessica knew it wasn't true. Elizabeth wasn't stuck-up at all. But she sure was stubborn.

CHAPTER 7

Valentine's Day Blues

"Who would like to help me pass out the cupcakes?" Mrs. Otis asked at the beginning of the last period.

Caroline Pearce instantly raised her hand. "I will!"

Mrs. Otis picked up the large, decorated box with all the class Valentine's Day cards in it. "I also need a volunteer to help me deliver these."

"Oh!" Caroline said, her hand shooting up again. "I'll do that!"

"You can't do everything, Caroline," Mrs.

Otis said, smiling. "Who else would like to help?"

Elizabeth raised her hand. "I will."

While everyone else rearranged the desks and began handing out napkins, cups, candies, and juice, Elizabeth opened the Valentine's Day "mail box." Inside were dozens of colorful cards. She picked out the first one. It was addressed to Andy Franklin.

"Somebody likes you," she told him, smiling.

Andy turned pink and quickly grabbed the card. Elizabeth knew it was from her. She had made valentines for almost everyone.

One by one, she passed out all the cards in the box. Each time she found one with her name on it, she hoped it would be in Jessica's handwriting. But none of them were. The card she had made for Jessica was in her notebook. Elizabeth had planned to give it to her during the party, but now she was beginning to worry. If Jessica wasn't going to give her a card, maybe she wouldn't give one to Jessica. Besides, she was still angry with Jessica for calling the Sunflower Club stupid.

"Thanks for the card you made me," Lois said, coming up to Elizabeth.

"You're welcome." Elizabeth glanced over at Jessica. Jessica was talking to Lila and Ellen, and she didn't look over. Seeing the silk orchids they were all wearing made Elizabeth even more upset.

"What's wrong?" Amy asked her. She was licking a giant heart-shaped lollipop.

"Nothing," Elizabeth said gloomily.

Eva sat down with them. "Did you see the

valentine that Charlie made for Mrs. Otis?" she asked with a grin. "There were globs of glue everywhere, but Mrs. Otis said it was the thought that counted."

"You could make up a funny poem about that," Amy said. "Roses are red, violets are blue, something something and something glue."

Eva and Amy both laughed, and they looked to see if Elizabeth would, too. But Elizabeth didn't.

"Are you and Jessica having a fight?" Eva asked at last.

Elizabeth shook her head. "I don't think so, but maybe we are. I didn't give her my card," she added in a low voice.

"You didn't?" Amy licked her lollipop and looked thoughtful. "Did she give you one?"

"No." Elizabeth nibbled some icing off her cupcake.

"Maybe she forgot," Eva said.

"Or maybe she'll give it to you later," Amy suggested.

"Maybe," Elizabeth agreed.

She looked over at Jessica again. It wasn't turning out to be a very nice Valentine's Day.

CHAPTER 8

No Fun

After school, almost everyone in the twins' class went to the park to play. Jessica, Lila, and Ellen weren't playing, though. They were just sitting on one of the benches.

"Let's go on the swings," Jessica suggested.

"No way, Vanilla," Lila said. "Look at how many Sunflowers are over there."

Jessica looked. "Oh. You're right." She watched as Elizabeth and Amy competed to see who could swing higher.

"When is your dad going on another trip, Lady's Slipper?" Ellen asked Lila. "Will he bring you some more souvenirs?"

Lila smiled proudly. "He's going to New York City soon," she said. "He said he'll bring me a miniature Statue of Liberty and a miniature Empire State Building."

Jessica wished Lila wouldn't brag so much about how many presents her father gave her. Almost the only thing the Orchid Club did now was listen to Lila show off.

"Do you want to play freeze tag?" Jessica asked her friends.

"No," Lila said, putting one hand over her silk orchid. "We'll ruin our flowers."

"We don't have enough people, anyway," Ellen said.

Jessica sighed. Near the slides, she could see that the Sunflowers had started a game of "Red Light, Green Light." It looked to her as if they were having a good time.

"If Elizabeth would join our club we'd have enough people for some games," Lila said.

"That's right," Ellen agreed. "Why won't she join?"

"I don't know," Jessica said, sounding grouchy.

"Does she think she's too good for us?" Lila asked.

Jessica shook her head angrily. "No! She just likes her dumb old Sunflowers better."

Jessica was upset with her sister for not joining the Orchid Club. But she was even more upset about not being able to play with Elizabeth. They were supposed to be best friends, but now Elizabeth played with the Sunflowers all the time, while Jessica sat with the Orchids. She was beginning to think that belonging to the Orchid Club wasn't very much fun after all.

She watched as the Sunflowers started playing TV tag. "Let's play *some*thing," Jessica begged her friends.

"Like what?" Ellen asked.

Lila shrugged. "I don't want to get my clothes messed up. I'm not going to do anything that will ruin my orchid, either."

Jessica looked over at the Sunflowers again. She watched gloomily as Elizabeth tagged Eva, making her "It." Eva screamed and started chasing Amy. "Oh, forget it," Jessica said suddenly, standing up.

"Where are you going?" Lila asked in surprise.

"You'll see," Jessica said as she marched away.

CHAPTER 9

Elizabeth's Plan

When Eva stumbled and fell down, she called a time-out. Elizabeth sat on the grass next to her, and Amy sat down with them to catch her breath.

"Look," Amy said. "Here comes Jessica."

Elizabeth looked over quickly. Jessica was walking toward them. Elizabeth hoped her sister was coming to join the Sunflower Club. She crossed her fingers behind her back.

"Hi," Jessica said shyly. Her hands were behind her back, too.

"Hi," Elizabeth said.

Jessica didn't say anything for a moment. "I forgot to give you this before," she blurted out suddenly, handing her sister a card.

Elizabeth took the card and opened it. Inside Jessica had drawn a picture of two blond-haired girls holding hands, with a large heart around them. Underneath it said, "Happy Valentine's Day. Love, Jessica."

"It's beautiful," Elizabeth said happily. She jumped up. "Wait here. I'll be right back!"

She dashed over to the bench where her jacket was and took the card she had made for Jessica out of the pocket. Then she ran back.

"Here," she said.

Jessica opened it and smiled. "Thanks, Liz. I'm sorry if you're sorry," she said.

"I'm sorry, too," Elizabeth said. She hugged Jessica.

"Can I be in the Sunflower Club?" Jessica asked. "Being in the Orchid Club is no fun. We never do anything."

Eva and Amy both laughed. "You need one special thing to get in," Eva said in a serious voice.

Jessica looked worried. "What?"

"A sunflower on your hand," Elizabeth said with a giggle. "Here."

She took a pen from her pocket and drew a sunflower on the back of her sister's hand. Jessica held it out for inspection.

"She's in," Amy announced.

"Is Jessica joining our club?" Lois asked as she ran over to see what was going on.

Elizabeth held Jessica's hand. "She sure is."

"Hey," Caroline called out. "Aren't we still playing TV tag?"

"Yes," Eva said. She stood up and immediately tagged Jessica. "Jessica's 'It.'"

Jessica laughed. "I'll get you!" She raced after Eva, and then dodged around the swing set to chase Elizabeth. Elizabeth was laughing so hard that she couldn't think of a television show to name, so Jessica was able to tag her.

It was much more fun to be in the Sunflower Club than in the Orchid Club, Jessica decided. The only rules she had to worry about were the rules of the game they were playing. She stopped by the seesaw to take a few deep breaths. Not far away, Lila and Ellen were pretending not to notice her.

"I wish they would join, too," Jessica said to Elizabeth. "They aren't having any fun. Running around wouldn't mess up their orchids, so it wouldn't matter if they played tag with us."

"Do you think they would join if you asked?" Elizabeth wondered.

Jessica shrugged. "Ellen would if Lila did. But you know Lila. She never wants to say she made a mistake."

Elizabeth thought for a minute. "I think I have an idea," she announced.

"You do?" Jessica's eyes sparkled. "What is it?"

Elizabeth put her hand to Jessica's ear to whisper. "This is what we do . . ."

CHAPTER 10

Kidnapped

Jessica tried to keep from smiling as she walked over to Lila and Ellen.

"Hi," she said, pretending to be casual.

"Hi, Vanilla," Ellen answered.

Lila frowned. "Don't call her that anymore. She can't be in the Orchid Club now. She's a Sunflower. Look at her hand."

Ellen shook her head when she saw the drawing on Jessica's hand. Jessica just grinned.

"I don't want to be in the Orchid Club anymore," she said. "I have a message for you from the Sunflowers."

"What?" Ellen asked, looking curious.

Lila folded her arms and put her nose in the air. "We don't want to know what it is."

Jessica knew that Lila would like being a Sunflower if she gave it a chance. But Lila was stubborn. She didn't like doing things she said she would never do.

"This is the message," Jessica said. "Surrender to the Sunflowers, or you will be kidnapped."

Ellen giggled. "Kidnapped? That sounds like fun."

"Shhh!" Lila said, shaking her head. "We're not going to surrender."

Ellen looked disappointed, but she didn't say anything.

"OK," Jessica said with a sigh. "But don't say we didn't warn you."

She walked back to where the Sunflowers were waiting.

"What did they say?" Amy asked with a giggle.

"Let me guess. I bet they won't surrender," Elizabeth said.

"Right," Jessica said. She looked over her shoulder at Ellen and Lila. Lila was ignoring them, but Ellen was watching.

Jessica knew that kidnapping her two friends was the perfect plan. That way, Lila and Ellen wouldn't have to surrender, but they could all be friends again.

"OK, spread out," Elizabeth said. "It's time for plan B."

Eva, Amy, Lois, Julie, Elizabeth, and Jessica began walking toward Ellen and Lila. When the last two Orchids saw the

Sunflowers coming they stood up and began to back away.

"We're going to get you!" Jessica said, trying not to laugh.

Ellen screamed and started running. The Sunflowers chased her and caught her. Ellen pretended to struggle, but then she stood still. "You got me," she said, smiling at Jessica.

"Quick, Eva. Draw a sunflower on her hand," Elizabeth said.

Eva drew a perfect sunflower on Ellen's hand. "There, you're in," Eva said. "Whether you like it or not."

"Now you can help us catch Lila," Jessica added.

Ellen looked at the drawing on her hand. "This is neat. We weren't having any fun being Orchids. Come on, let's get her!"

The Sunflowers began marching toward Lila. Lila's eyes became very round. "You let them catch you, Ellen!" she called out. "You're not an Orchid anymore!"

"Surrender, Lila!" Jessica said. "This is your last chance!"

Lila looked around her. There were smiling Sunflowers on every side. Jessica could see that Lila was trying not to look as if she was having a good time.

"OK, if that's the way you want it," Jessica said, dashing toward her friend.

"No!" Lila screamed. But she laughed when Jessica began tickling her. "No fair!"

In a moment, everyone was tickling Lila, and Lila was giggling nonstop. "I give up! I give up!" Lila gasped. "I'll be a Sunflower!" She held out her hand so that Eva could draw a sunflower on it.

"We knew you would," Elizabeth said. "Now we can play freeze tag again. And Lila's 'It'!"

After playing tag for a while, all of the Sunflowers sat down to rest in the shade.

"Whew, it's hot," Jessica said, wiping the sweat off her forehead. "I wish I didn't have to ride my bike home."

"Do you want a taxi to come pick you up?" Elizabeth asked, smiling.

Jessica shook her head. "I want a limousine. Somebody here gets picked up in one all the time."

"Oh, I know who that is," Lila said. She made a face. "It's Bruce Patman. He's in third grade."

"Is he rich?" Eva asked.

"Yes," Lila said. "He's spoiled rotten. He gets to have anything he wants."

Jessica put her hand over her mouth to hide a smile. Lila was spoiled rotten, too. Her parents always bought her everything she asked for.

"Look, there he is," Lila said. "I call him Mr. Stuck-Up."

Jessica looked where Lila was pointing. Bruce Patman was sitting on a brand-new BMX bike near the park gates. A long black limousine stopped in front of him, and a man wearing a blue uniform and a matching cap got out of the driver's seat. The man opened the back door and held it while Bruce got into the back seat. Bruce left his bicycle where it was on the sidewalk, and after shutting the car door the driver put it in the trunk.

"He looks like a real snob," Amy said.

Jessica nodded in agreement.

Is Bruce Patman as rotten as everybody says? Find out in Sweet Valley Kids #27, THE SWEET VALLEY CLEANUP TEAM.

SWEET VALLEY KIDS

Jessica and Elizabeth have had lots of adventures in *Sweet Valley High* and *Sweet Valley Twins*...now read about the twins at age seven! You'll love all the fun that comes with being seven—birthday parties, playing dress-up, class projects, putting on puppet shows and plays, losing a tooth, setting up lemonade stands, caring for animals and much more! It's all part of SWEET VALLEY KIDS. Read them all!

☐ **JESSICA AND THE SPELLING BEE SURPRISE #21**   15917-8 $2.75

☐ **SWEET VALLEY SLUMBER PARTY #22**   15934-8 $2.75

☐ **LILA'S HAUNTED HOUSE PARTY # 23**   15919-4 $2.99

☐ **COUSIN KELLY'S FAMILY SECRET # 24**   15920-8 $2.75

☐ **LEFT-OUT ELIZABETH # 25**   15921-6 $2.99

☐ **JESSICA'S SNOBBY CLUB # 26**   15922-4 $2.99

☐ **THE SWEET VALLEY CLEANUP TEAM # 27**   15923-2 $2.99

☐ **ELIZABETH MEETS HER HERO #28**   15924-0 $2.99

☐ **ANDY AND THE ALIEN # 29**   15925-9 $2.99

☐ **JESSICA'S UNBURIED TREASURE # 30**   15926-7 $2.99

SWEET VALLEY KIDS

Jessica and Elizabeth have had lots of adventures in *Sweet Valley High* and *Sweet Valley Twins*...now read about the twins at age seven! You'll love all the fun that comes with being seven—birthday parties, playing dress-up, class projects, putting on puppet shows and plays, losing a tooth, setting up lemonade stands, caring for animals and much more! It's all part of SWEET VALLEY KIDS. Read them all!

☐	SURPRISE! SURPRISE! #1	15758-2	$2.75/$3.25
☐	RUNAWAY HAMSTER #2	15759-0	$2.75/$3.25
☐	THE TWINS' MYSTERY TEACHER # 3	15760-4	$2.75/$3.25
☐	ELIZABETH'S VALENTINE # 4	15761-2	$2.99/$3.50
☐	JESSICA'S CAT TRICK # 5	15768-X	$2.75/$3.25
☐	LILA'S SECRET # 6	15773-6	$2.75/$3.25
☐	JESSICA'S BIG MISTAKE # 7	15799-X	$2.75/$3.25
☐	JESSICA'S ZOO ADVENTURE # 8	15802-3	$2.75/$3.25
☐	ELIZABETH'S SUPER-SELLING LEMONADE #9	15807-4	$2.99/$3.50
☐	THE TWINS AND THE WILD WEST #10	15811-2	$2.75/$3.25
☐	CRYBABY LOIS #11	15818-X	$2.99/$3.50
☐	SWEET VALLEY TRICK OR TREAT #12	15825-2	$2.75/$3.25
☐	STARRING WINSTON EGBERT #13	15836-8	$2.75/$3.25
☐	JESSICA THE BABY-SITTER #14	15838-4	$2.75/$3.25
☐	FEARLESS ELIZABETH #15	15844-9	$2.75/$3.25
☐	JESSICA THE TV STAR #16	15850-3	$2.75/$3.25
☐	CAROLINE'S MYSTERY DOLLS #17	15870-8	$2.75/$3.25
☐	BOSSY STEVEN #18	15881-3	$2.75/$3.25
☐	JESSICA AND THE JUMBO FISH #19	15936-4	$2.99/$3.50
☐	THE TWINS GO TO THE HOSPITAL #20	15912-7	$2.99/$3.50
☐	THE CASE OF THE SECRET SANTA (SVK Super Snooper #1)	15860-0	$2.95/$3.50
☐	THE CASE OF THE MAGIC CHRISTMAS BELL (SVK Super Snooper #2)	15964-X	$2.99/$3.50

Buy them at your local bookstore or use this handy page for ordering:

Bantam Books, Dept. SVT3, 2451 S. Wolf Road, Des Plaines, IL 60018

Please send me the items I have checked above. I am enclosing $_____
(please add $2.50 to cover postage and handling). Send check or money
order, no cash or C.O.D.s please.

Mr/Ms _____

Address _____

City/State _____ Zip _____

SVT3-4/92

Please allow four to six weeks for delivery.
Prices and availability subject to change without notice.